I0815351

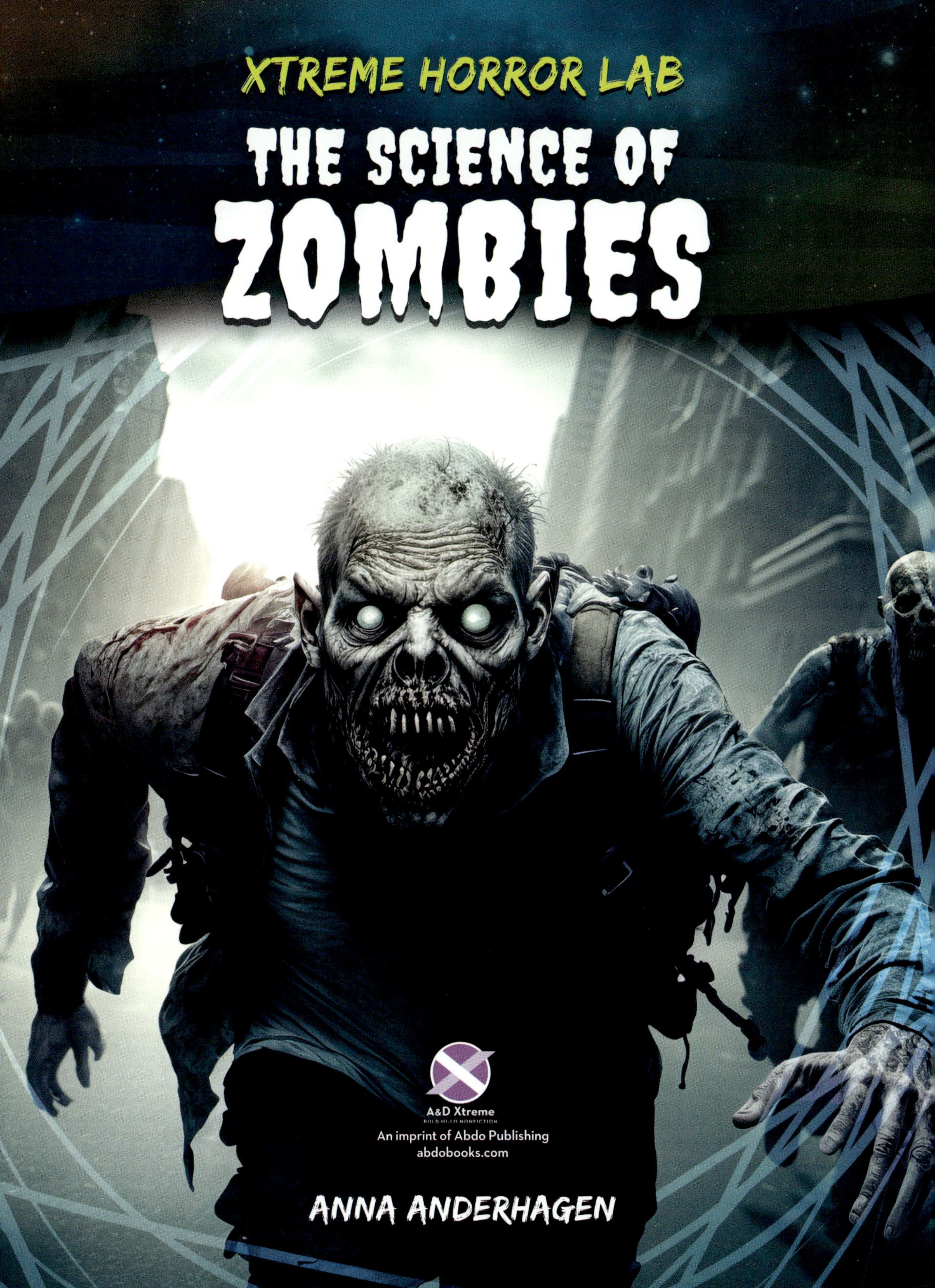
XTREME HORROR LAB
THE SCIENCE OF
ZOMBIES
A&D Xtreme
An imprint of Abdo Publishing
abdobooks.com
ANNA ANDERHAGEN

TAKE IT TO THE XTREME!

GET READY FOR AN EXTREME ADVENTURE! THE PAGES OF THIS BOOK WILL TAKE YOU INTO THE SPOOKY WORLD OF UNEXPLAINED PHENOMENA. WHEN YOU HAVE FINISHED READING THIS BOOK, TAKE THE XTREME CHALLENGE ON PAGE 43 ABOUT WHAT YOU'VE LEARNED!

ABDOBOOKS.COM
Published by Abdo Publishing, a division of ABDO, PO Box 398166, Minneapolis, Minnesota 55439.

Printed in the United States of America, North Mankato, MN.
052024
092024

Design: Kelly Doudna, Mighty Media, Inc.
Production: Mighty Media, Inc.
Editor: Jessica Rusick
Cover Photograph: ink drop/Adobe Stock
Interior Photographs: Album/Alamy Photo, pp. 26–27; Anthony Karen/Wikimedia Commons, pp. 16–17; Aonprom Photo/Shutterstock Images, pp. 38–39; Bogdan Dyiakonovych/Shutterstock Images, pp. 18–19; CDC/Wikimedia Commons, pp. 40–41; Davis, Robert Hobart/Wikimedia Commons, p. 19; Dmytro/Adobe Stock, p. 44; 4zevar/Adobe Stock, p. 45; FtLaud/Shutterstock Images, pp. 32–33; gabrielsarabando/Shutterstock Images, pp. 14–15; ink drop/Adobe Stock, p. 1; Jean-Claude FRANCOLON/Getty Images, pp. 30–31; John Zada/Alamy Photo, p. 35; Jordan/Adobe Stock, pp. 8–9; Keitma/Adobe Stock, pp. 4–5, 24–25; Kiselev Andrey Valerevich/Shutterstock Images, pp. 6–7; LFRabanedo/Shutterstock Images, pp. 36–37; Pictorial Parade/Wikimedia Commons, p. 23; Romolo Tavani/Shutterstock Images, p. 42; Sean Dudley/Wikimedia Commons, pp. 22–23; Stanislau Beloglazov/Adobe Stock, pp. 34–35; Steve Allen Travel & Wildlife Photography/Adobe Stock, pp. 12–13; Sylvie Corriveau/Shutterstock Images, pp. 28–29; WENN Rights Ltd/Alamy Photo, pp. 10–11; Wikimedia Commons, pp. 20–21
Design Elements: Dominik Hladik/Shutterstock Images (moon); nikiteev_konstantin/Shutterstock Images (curves); pixelparticle/Shutterstock Images (stars); pixssa/Shutterstock Images (stretchy circle)

LIBRARY OF CONGRESS CONTROL NUMBER: 2023949418

PUBLISHER'S CATALOGING-IN-PUBLICATION DATA
Names: Anderhagen, Anna, author.
Title: The science of zombies / by Anna Anderhagen
Description: Minneapolis, Minnesota : Abdo Publishing, 2025 | Series: Xtreme horror lab | Includes online resources and index.
Identifiers: ISBN 9781098293253 (lib. bdg.) | ISBN 9798384912521 (ebook)
Subjects: LCSH: Zombies--Juvenile literature. | Monsters--Juvenile literature. | Zombies in popular culture--Juvenile literature. | Science--Juvenile literature.
Classification: DDC 130--dc23

TABLE OF CONTENTS

CHAPTER 1

ROTTING FLESH

You are walking home at night. You see a group of people walking slowly toward you with outstretched arms. They are dragging their feet and moaning. As they get closer, you notice they have red eyes and rotting flesh. One **lunges** toward you! You scream and wake up from your zombie nightmare.

Many horror stories and movies involve humans working together to survive as zombies take over the world.

CHAPTER 2

TERRIFYING TERMINOLOGY

A zombie is a type of **supernatural** being. Zombies are undead. This means they live after dying. Legends claim zombies rise out of graves. Sometimes they attack humans. Zombies are said to walk slowly. They have little control over their muscles. Their skin may look like it is rotting.

In many stories, zombies do not get tired. They are violent beings who will stop at nothing to eat human flesh.

Many cultures have legends of zombie-like beings. They are all different. In some African and Caribbean cultures, zombies do not eat people. Instead, they are **enslaved** to their keepers. These zombies are mindless beings who do not have **free will**.

According to some legends, people can free an enslaved zombie by feeding it salt. This is said to return the zombie to its right mind.

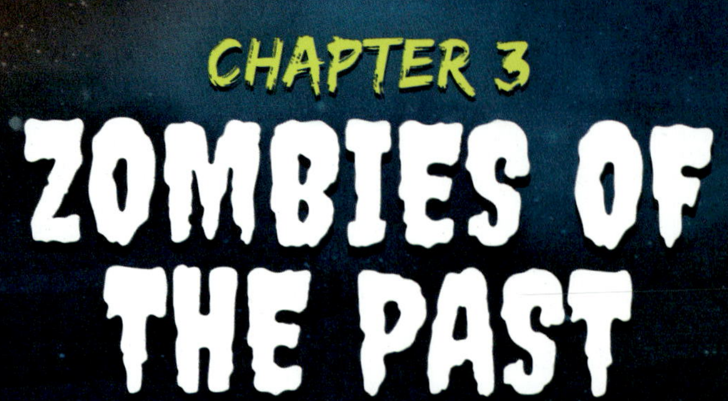

CHAPTER 3
ZOMBIES OF THE PAST

The ancient Greeks believed dead people could rise out of graves and harm the living. The ancient Greeks buried dead bodies deep in the ground to stop them from rising. They also pinned dead bodies down with rocks or stakes.

Archaeologists have discovered several staked skeletons in Bulgaria. The graves date back to the Middle Ages.

Broken and burnt skeleton remains were found in the medieval village of Wharram Percy, England. Archaeologists believe the damage was done to prevent the dead from rising.

In the **Middle Ages**, people believed evil spirits could possess dead bodies and bring them back to life. Archaeologists in Ireland have found skeletons with large rocks in their mouths. These date back to 700 CE. Similar discoveries have been made in other European countries. The rocks were meant to stop spirits from entering the bodies.

CHAPTER 4
ZOMBIES & VODOU

The term "zombie" comes from the vodou religion of West Africa. People mainly practice vodou in the Caribbean and other places with African **heritage**. Most people who practice vodou believe zombies are a myth. But some people believe vodou priests can create zombies.

The African country Benin is one of the birthplaces of vodou. The country has a national vodou holiday that is celebrated with dances and rituals.

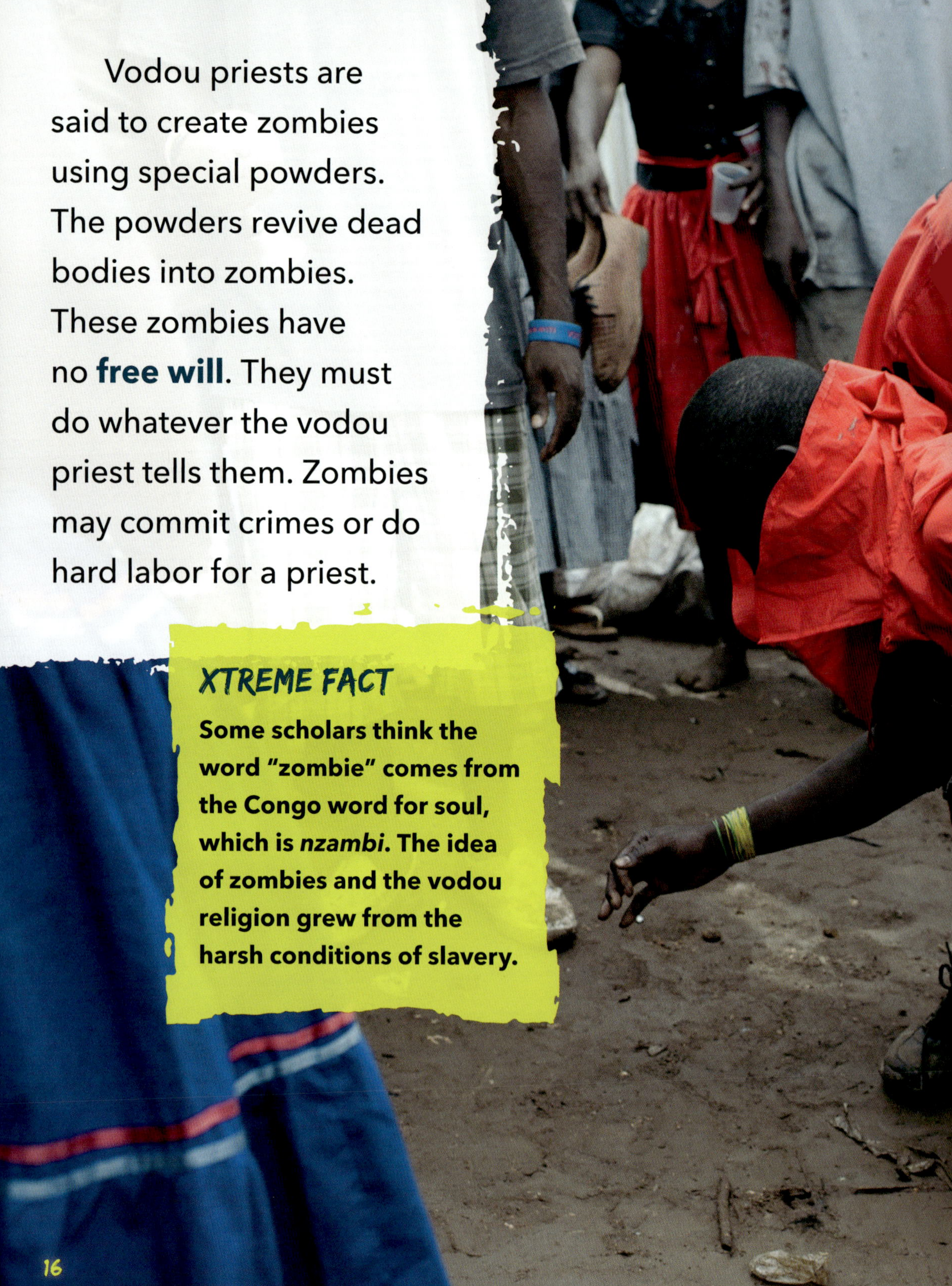

Vodou priests are said to create zombies using special powders. The powders revive dead bodies into zombies. These zombies have no **free will**. They must do whatever the vodou priest tells them. Zombies may commit crimes or do hard labor for a priest.

XTREME FACT

Some scholars think the word "zombie" comes from the Congo word for soul, which is *nzambi*. The idea of zombies and the vodou religion grew from the harsh conditions of slavery.

A Haitian vodou ceremony. Male vodou priests are known as *oungan* or *houngan*. Male vodou priests who harm others are known as a *bòkò* or *bokor*.

CHAPTER 5

ZOMBIES IN POPULAR CULTURE

Zombie stories started to become popular in 1929. That year, explorer William Seabrook published a book called *The Magic Island*. It was a travel book describing zombies in Haiti within the vodou religion. Soon after it was published, people began making movies about zombies. In these movies, the zombies had no **free will**.

William Seabrook wrote *The Magic Island* after traveling to Haiti. There, he met a vodou priestess. She showed him several vodou rituals, which he included in his book.

Haiti gets its name from the Arawak word *Ayti*, which means "mountainous land." The uneven terrain found here is some of the roughest in the Caribbean Islands.

Movie zombies began to change in the 1950s. They became monsters who attacked people. They were also more violent and **gruesome**. These zombies shared few similarities with vodou zombies.

White Zombie, a film based on *The Magic Island*, was the first feature-length horror film about zombies.

The zombie movie *Night of the Living Dead* came out in 1968. It caused zombies to grow even more popular! The movie inspired many modern zombie films. In most modern zombie movies, zombies are undead. They are covered in blood and have rotting skin.

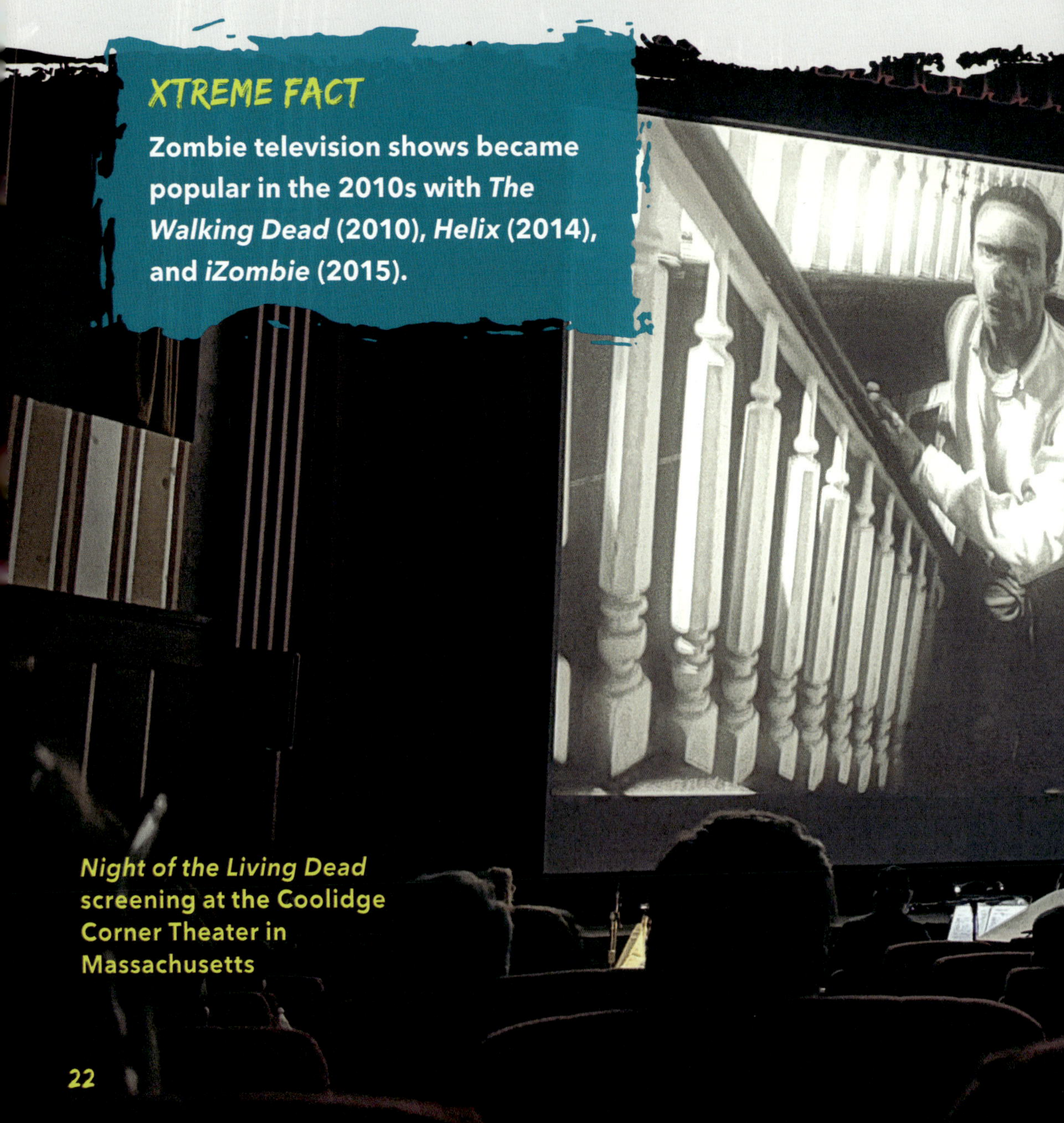

XTREME FACT

Zombie television shows became popular in the 2010s with *The Walking Dead* (2010), *Helix* (2014), and *iZombie* (2015).

Night of the Living Dead screening at the Coolidge Corner Theater in Massachusetts

Night of the Living Dead grossed $12 million in the US and $18 million internationally. More than five sequels were released between 1978 and 2009.

Modern zombies want to attack humans. Their mission is to feed on human flesh. They usually leave animals alone. Zombies can be violent and **persistent**. They can survive severe injuries. They only die if their brains or heads are removed.

Experts who study zombie portrayals in popular culture believe zombies symbolize different fears. These fears include death, the loss of free will, and the end of the world.

Few people today connect zombies with vodou. Modern stories tell of space **radiation** or a virus turning people into zombies. A person can also turn into a zombie if bitten by one.

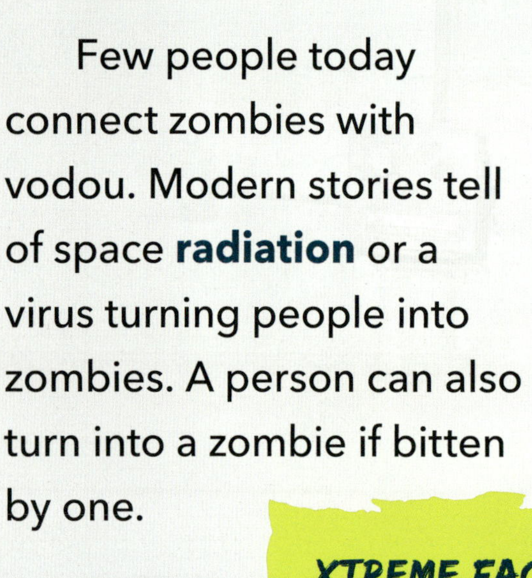

XTREME FACT

There is a fungus that turns ants into zombies! Ants eat the fungus. The fungus grows inside the ant. As it grows, the ant loses control of its body. The fungus makes the ant move to a warm location where the fungus can thrive. Then it kills the ant.

In the popular video game and TV show *The Last of Us*, a fungal infection turns humans into zombies.

CHAPTER 6

A REAL ZOMBIE STORY?

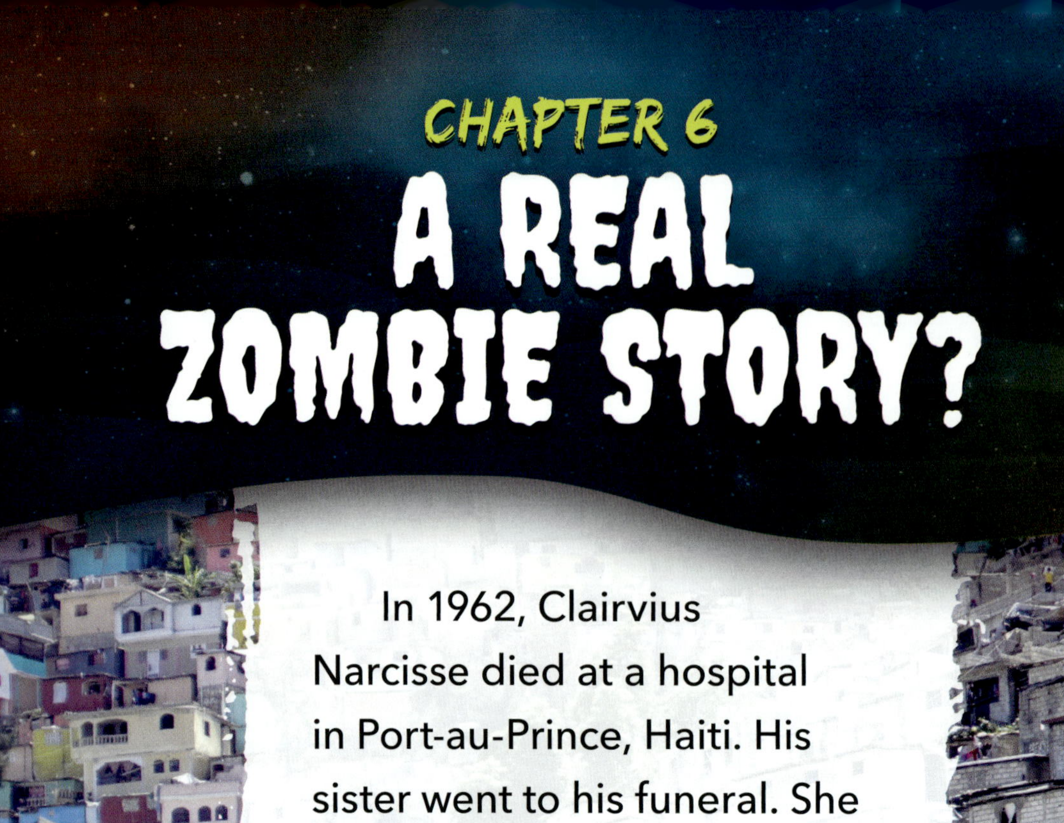

In 1962, Clairvius Narcisse died at a hospital in Port-au-Prince, Haiti. His sister went to his funeral. She watched her brother's body be buried. Eighteen years later, Narcisse found his sister at a village marketplace! He said he had been buried alive and dug up by a vodou priest.

Port-au-Prince is the capital of Haiti and the country's largest city. Most Port-au-Prince residents live on small incomes.

Narcisse at his burial site. He said that he and the other zombies could only escape the sugar plantation after the vodou priest died.

Narcisse showed his sister the scar on his right cheek from the nail closing his coffin. Many people who lived in the village identified him. Narcisse said a vodou priest forced him and other zombies to work on a sugar plantation.

CHAPTER 7

SCIENTIFIC EXPLANATIONS

Scientist Wade Davis researched Narcisse's story along with other zombie stories. He also researched the zombie powders that vodou priests use. He learned the powders contain herbs, shells, hair, and animal bones. Many also contain a poison called tetrodotoxin. Tetrodotoxin can cause zombie-like symptoms in people. These include difficulty walking, **paralysis**, and **coma**.

Tetrodotoxin is commonly found inside pufferfish. The poison shuts down the nervous system. This can stop things such as muscular functions and breathing.

Davis learned that vodou priests rub tetrodotoxin powder into the skin of a victim. Within hours, the victim can hardly breathe and becomes **paralyzed**. The heartbeat slows so much it can't be heard. The victim appears dead and may then be buried alive. Later, a vodou priest can dig up the victim.

Objects used in vodou rituals

Davis (*pictured*) met with a vodou priest in Saint Marc, Haiti. The priest made Davis a powder using parts of toads, sea worms, lizards, tarantulas, and human bones.

Jimson weed is also known as devil's snare or thorn apple. It has been used as an herbal medicine and can be eaten, smoked, or made into tea.

After digging up the body, the vodou priest gives the victim another drug. It is made from Jimson weed. Jimson weed causes confusion and memory loss. These symptoms make it easy for someone to control a victim.

Zombie legends may also be explained by various illnesses. One is a rare mental illness called Cotard's syndrome. People with this syndrome think they are dead and **decomposing**. They may complain that they smell like rotting flesh and want to be with dead people. They believe their brain and other organs have stopped working.

People with Cotard's syndrome also often struggle with depression.

Many zombies may have been people with rabies. Rabies is a disease transmitted through the rabies virus. People get the virus after being bitten by an **infected** animal, such as a bat or dog. Many rabies symptoms are similar to zombie behavior. These include increased **aggression** and a desire to bite.

XTREME FACT

Yaws is a bacterial infection that affects a human's skin and bones. It causes zombie-like sores over a person's face and body. It also causes the bones to swell.

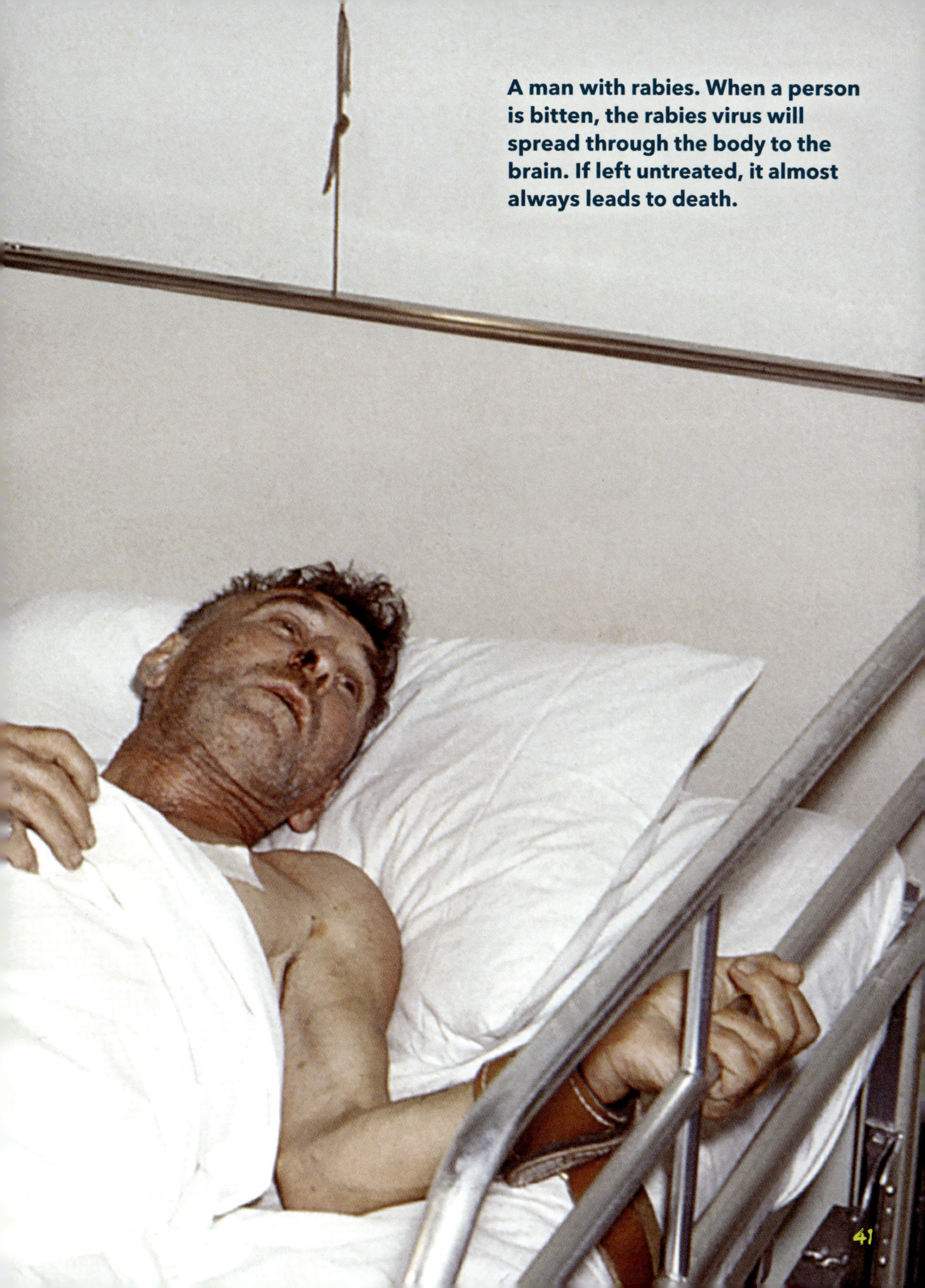

A man with rabies. When a person is bitten, the rabies virus will spread through the body to the brain. If left untreated, it almost always leads to death.

CHAPTER 8

SCIENCE VS. STORIES

Zombie stories have **evolved** over hundreds of years. The stories often tried to explain the fear of human death or strange human behavior. Science can now explain the facts behind these myths. But zombie stories are still here today. Do you believe in zombies?

XTREME CHALLENGE

TAKE THE QUIZ BELOW AND PUT WHAT YOU'VE LEARNED TO THE TEST!

1) What is a zombie?

2) Why do you think people believed in zombies?

3) How are zombies connected to the vodou religion?

4) What diseases are associated with zombies?

5) After reading this book, do you believe in zombies?

ZOMBIE HORROR LAB

In many stories, zombies have rotting flesh. Try this experiment to learn about skin and how it rots.

WHAT YOU NEED

- 2 tomatoes of equal size with no bruises or breaks in the skin
- plate or tray
- toothpick
- pencil and paper
- magnifying glass

WHAT YOU DO

1. Put the tomatoes on the plate or tray.
2. Poke at least five holes in one of the tomatoes with a toothpick. Leave the other tomato alone.
3. Keep the tomatoes on the tray at room temperature. Make sure they are not disturbed.

4 Watch the tomatoes every day for at least seven days. Record what you see and smell. Do the poked and unpoked tomatoes look the same? Does the color, smell, texture, and shape change over time?

5 Use a magnifying glass to look carefully at the surfaces of the tomatoes. What do you see? Do you notice any rotting in the tomatoes? Where?

WHAT HAPPENED?

Notice that the poked tomato skin has likely shrunk and rotted. You may find fungi or other microorganisms attacking it. Your skin is very similar to the tomato skin. It acts as a barrier to prevent viruses, bacteria, and other microorganisms from entering your body. Poking the tomato skin with the toothpick creates holes that allow microorganisms to enter the tomato. As they invade the tomato, the microorganisms multiply and rot the tomato.

GLOSSARY

aggression–forceful or hostile actions.

coma–a condition resembling deep sleep that is caused by sickness or injury.

decompose–to break down into simpler parts.

enslave–to force someone to do labor under the threat of violence.

evolve–to develop gradually.

free will–the ability to make one's own choices.

gruesome–causing disgust and horror.

heritage–a tradition or practice that is handed down from the past.

infected–to have a disease caused by bacteria or other germs. Such a sickness is an infection.

lunge–to leap or jump forward suddenly.

Middle Ages–a period in European history that lasted from about 500 CE to about 1500 CE.

paralysis—the loss of motion or feeling in a part of the body. Someone experiencing paralysis is paralyzed.

persistent—continuing to do something despite obstacles or resistance.

radiation—energy particles that are given off by something.

supernatural—relating to magic, spirits, or other things that cannot be explained by science or nature.

ONLINE RESOURCES

To learn more about zombies, please visit **abdobooklinks.com** or scan this QR code. These links are routinely monitored and updated to provide the most current information available.

INDEX